The Ugly Duckling

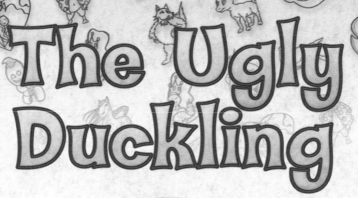

Adapted by Larry Carney
Illustrated by Paul McGill

PC Multimedia Entertainment
TREASURES, INC.

Published by

PC Multimedia Entertainment
TREASURES, INC.

1795 N. Lapeer Rd., Oxford, Michigan 48371 USA

The Ugly Duckling

Adapted by Larry Carney
Illustrated by Paul McGill
Audio CD Reading Performed by David DuChene
Songs Written by Larry Carney
Songs Produced and Performed by D. B. Harris

ISBN 1-60072-033-1

First Published 2007

Made in China.

Once upon a time there was a farm in the country filled with happy barnyard animals. There were galloping horses, mud-splattered pigs, munching goats, clucking chickens, and grazing cows and sheep.

At the edge of the farmyard was a pond lined with cattails and reeds. The mother ducks swam happily around the pond, and in the spring they made nests along the shore in which to lay and warm their eggs.

Each day the mommy ducks would talk happily to one another about the dreams they had for their little ducklings once they hatched.

One of the mommy ducks, Mrs. Waddle, was especially excited about her eggs and very eager for them to hatch. She knew that one of her eggs was very special.

Living in the most beautiful section at the edge of the pond was Mrs. Quack, the oldest and most respected of all the ducks on the farm. Each year Mrs. Quack would visit with the sitting mothers and remark on their nests and eggs.

"Oh, what a lovely nest!" she said as she visited with Mrs. Waddle. "And let's have a look at your eggs."

Mrs. Waddle stood up proudly to show Mrs. Quack her clutch of five fine eggs.

Mrs. Quack peered closely at one egg that was much larger and darker than the others and said sternly, "Why Mrs. Waddle, whatever is that?"

Mrs. Waddle looked at the egg lovingly and said, "Yes, it's quite different. Isn't it wonderful?"

Mrs. Quack responded, "It isn't wonderful at all! It looks to me like a turkey's egg!"

Mrs. Waddle was very upset by Mrs. Quack's rude comments and replied glumly, "But…how could that be?"

"Oh, it happens sometimes. Some lazy turkey sneaks up and puts one of their eggs in your nest when you're not looking. Just roll it out of the nest and don't waste your time hatching this outsider."

Mrs. Waddle smiled and said quietly, "Thank you kindly for your advice, but I've been sitting on this egg as long as all the others and I will continue to do just that."

Mrs. Quack was offended by having her advice ignored and stormed off.

A few days later, eggs began hatching all around the little pond and the air was filled with the cheerful quacks of the fuzzy baby ducklings.

Mrs. Waddle watched with a cheerful heart as her little ducklings hatched. One by one they came, each one a beautiful, downy little duckling, until the only egg left in the nest was the large dark one. Mrs. Waddle gave the remaining egg a gentle nudge with her bill, anxious for it to hatch. Suddenly, the egg began to wiggle and a big crack appeared. Soon the shell split in two and to her amazement Mrs. Waddle saw…

…the cutest little ugly duckling she had ever seen. It had a long, skinny neck and big round eyes that bulged out of its fat head. Its feet and legs were awkward and far too big for its body, and it was covered in patches of dark gray down. It looked up at its mother with great love in its eyes and let out a tremendous "HONK!"

The other ducklings were startled by the loud
noise and hid behind their mother. Mrs. Waddle
gazed lovingly at the ugly duckling and with a
tender smile pulled it close to her warm body.
This ugly duckling was as beautiful and as dear
to Mrs. Waddle as each of her other ducklings.
All afternoon and into the evening Mrs.
Waddle snuggled and cuddled her little ones,
though her other little ducklings kept their
distance from their homely sibling.

The next morning all of the ducklings gathered around the bank of the little pond as their mothers watched from a distance. The water was very inviting, but the ducklings were all a little nervous about their first swim. Mrs. Waddle led her ducklings to the pond and watched proudly as they wobbled down to the water's edge. The little ugly duckling came down last. It was so much bigger and different from the rest of them that the other ducklings didn't know what to make of it.

Mrs. Waddle joined the other mother ducks.
She said, "Good morning," to them but they
turned up their bills and stepped away from her.
Mrs. Waddle was confused by this rude behavior
and asked, "Have I done something wrong?"

"You certainly have!" said Mrs. Quack as
she waddled her way through the crowd.

She pointed at the ugly duckling and said sternly, "Why would you would bring that ugly duckling out in public? You have shamed all of us." Mrs. Waddle was hurt by Mrs. Quack's unkind words. She loved all her ducklings dearly and would never feel embarrassed by any of them.

Mrs. Waddle became alarmed when she saw
all the other ducklings gathering in a circle
around her little ugly duckling. They were all
quacking and laughing and calling it names.
The poor ugly duckling started crying and
called out for its mother. Mrs. Waddle ran
down to the ugly duckling and put a protective
wing around it. "Stop it!" she quacked loudly.
"You should all be ashamed of yourselves!"
She quickly gathered her other ducklings
and took them back to her nest.

Mrs. Waddle made her other ducklings apologize to the ugly duckling and she did her best to comfort it. "Come, come," she said to her sobbing duckling, "it's alright. I'll make sure that they won't tease you again." The ugly duckling said sadly, "I'm not crying because they picked on me. I'm crying because I saw my reflection in the pond. I really am ugly!"

Mrs. Waddle pulled the ugly duckling closer and said softly, "You are not ugly at all. You are special, and I love you. I wouldn't change you for anything." But the ugly duckling cried the rest of the day and well into the night.

TURN PAGE

The next morning Mrs. Waddle began to lead her ducklings down to the pond, but the ugly duckling refused to go. Mrs. Waddle did her motherly best to convince the duckling to join the family at the pond, but finally agreed that the ugly duckling could remain in the nest.

The ugly duckling sat alone. All it could think of was how different and unwelcome it was. After much thought, it decided to go off on its own and wandered sadly across the farmyard.

As it waddled down the path to the other side of the farmyard, the ugly little duckling was teased by all of the animals it passed. It kept its head down and continued walking. Eventually, the duckling came to the edge of the farmyard where there was a muddy little pool of water. The ugly duckling waddled into the water and stayed there.

Spring turned into summer, and the ugly duckling never left its lonely little pond. Whenever another animal would come by it would hide its head underwater until they passed. Once the ugly duckling heard his mother's warm voice nearby. Although it missed her terribly, it stayed hidden until she went away. Every day the ugly duckling remembered how the other ducklings teased it. It remembered the sight of its ugly reflection in the water and was careful to not look into the water to see that ugly reflection again.

Fall came and the air grew colder. As winter approached the ugly duckling worked to stay warm by paddling quickly about the nearly frozen pond. The winter months were harsh with heavy snows and icy winds, and the ugly duckling could barely find enough to eat.

Finally, spring came. Warm sunshine filled the sky and the scent of wild flowers floated on the warm breezes. The ugly duckling swam with ease around the muddy pond and ate its fill of fresh grass. It felt joy at the arrival of the new season and happily splashed about the pond. Then, the ugly duckling saw its reflection in the water.

It stopped swimming and stared at this wonderful reflection. The ugly duckling was amazed. It tilted its head, and the reflection did the same. It opened its bill and winked an eye and the reflection did the same. The poor ugly duckling had grown into the most beautiful bird in the barnyard! It spread its graceful wings and flew joyfully to the duck pond.

Mrs. Waddle wept tears of joy when she recognized her long-lost child, now a beautiful swan. "Oh my dear one, you've come back to me!" she exclaimed.

"Mother look…I'm not ugly anymore!" said the swan.

Mrs. Waddle replied lovingly, "My dear, dear child, you were never ugly to me."

Collect Them ALL!

Goldilocks and the Three Bears

Hansel and Gretel

Little Red Riding Hood

The Gingerbread Man

The Little Mermaid

The Three Little Pigs

The Ugly Duckling

Cinderella

Plus Many More

See them all and much more at www.FairyTalePop.com

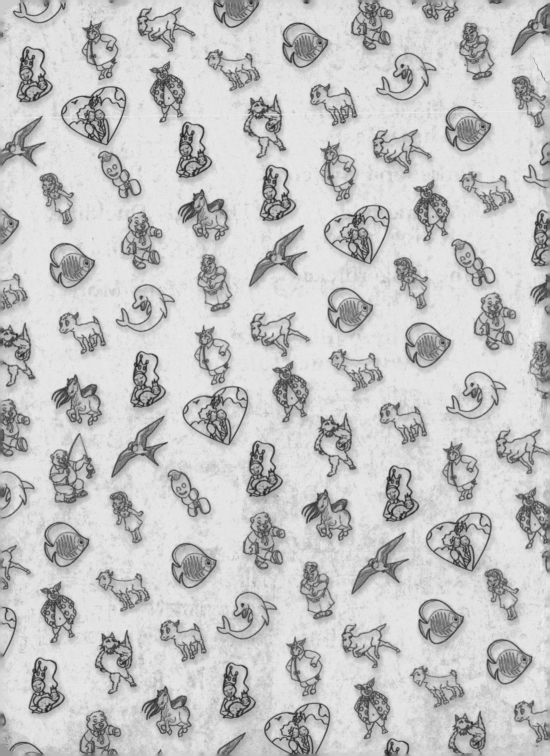